# Four Short Stories

## Thomas Jobling

This, my fourth book, is dedicated to my
wonderful, beautiful but late grandson,


Stan.


In every minute of every day you inspire me.
I miss you wee man.

# FIRST TIMER

# Anticipation

Darren's in the bathroom – has been for near on an hour. It's gone six-thirty. Upstairs an aged and poorly fitted door has become framed by an outpouring of illuminated steam. Below, iPads and similar tablets are wound up to full volume while frustrated faces are focused heavenwards. Nothing but nothing can quell the cacophony of nail-scratching toneless lyrics oozing out and tumbling down the bare wooden staircase.

"Shine ohhhh yeah shine..."

"Like a... ohhh… yeah..."

"So beautiful, beautiful Shine br..."

The thumping on ceilings has failed to drown out Darren's rhythm-less chanting. On the floor below, his co-renters are corpsed. Gillian is bent-double with bladder issues. Eric and Darren's brother, Francie, likewise, they also have fingers stuffed into their ears. In unison, out goes a final call, "Oh, for pity's sake Darren, give us a break son."

Unaware of the hullabaloo below, his bony probing finger calmly shuts down the electric shower. Vigorously he dries himself then wipes away the layer of condensation from a mirrored cabinet, which hangs precariously above a cracked sink. A blurred image demands attention; staring back he wonders; *umm, a bit wrinkled but I'm clean. Pears clean? Perhaps a bit too clean and maybe, bit smelly as in, girly smelly?* The opening of the cabinet has revealed a veritable treasure chest of potions, mostly Gillian's. Then he spots his big brother's man-sized 'Lynx Excite' body spray. Holding the canister at arm's length he declares; "Yeah, that'll do the job. Spray it on." At this point his inner voice chirps up; *yeah spray it all over, and do a double dose for the curly bits down below son.*

Next on Darren's ablutions journey is his spot-squeezing ritual. It's the start of the endgame – styling of wet hair and the fixing of it with a party-sized dollop of gel. The body beautifying phase ends with a bold declaration towards that misty reflection. "Darren, you are … one good lookin' guy." He rubs an eyebrow while wrapping himself in a towel that has seen better days.

A sharp crack from the bathroom door's barrel bolt ricochets around the crumbling mid-terrace lodgings. Like a starting pistol it also signals the start of a toilet stampede. Darren meanwhile, towel coming adrift, bounds from bathroom to bedroom. Leading the charge is Gillian who is afforded more of a view of

Darren's private 'profile' that perhaps she should have! But as for him, only one thought lingers – that of seeing *her* tonight.

Within the privacy of his room the evening's dressing plan kicks in; style choices and colour combinations; pants, socks, shirt...

# Action Stations

Having parked his suspension-lowered big-bore-exhaust hatch-back conveniently close to the venue, Darren tentatively approaches the hotel's revolving door. Rigid with anticipation, he pauses within the foyer. His eyes scan the seasonal gathering for a friendly face. Shoulders straight, he centres his loosely knotted tie. He brushes the draping arms of his navy suit. It's the same routine for the trousers. They, unlike the arms of his suit are perhaps a little shorter than he would like, however they do show off his festive socks. With a nervous swagger he enters the domain of this ... his first office party.

Conspicuously playing with his keys which are securely hooked around his little finger he is on one hand, masking nerves while on the other, transmitting a signal. A few weeks ago Darren had ditched his 'L' plates so this office party is offering a perfect opportunity to get that passenger seat of his little red Ford occupied. *Yep I've got the equipment to pull the babes ... one in particular! So, bring it on.*

Using every inch of his six foot something frame he casts a further searching eye. But Darren has only one face to find: *Oh great, she's here.* Whitney! *She's over there! She's waving. Waving at me? Is she waving to me? Yes she is!*

"Jeepers, what do I do now?" he asks aloud.

"Sorry? What—?" asks a voice standing shoulder-to-shoulder on his right side?

"Oh, oh nothing mate— just thinking out loud— sorry."

Within the milling crowd he has become aware of a tall girl standing close to his left. It was the white framed glasses that caught his attention. He nodded, she smiled sending him a quizzical glance. Tongue-tied his eyes danced nervously. A further glance back over his shoulder confirms that the tall girl with the white spectacles remains close by. His response is a cheeky lad-ish smirk. Quickly this juvenile train of thought gets parked as he remembers who he is planning to meet up with.

Darren's vulnerability, indecision and general inexperience with matters of romance have been laid bare. Shoulders now drooped he is nevertheless thinking fast. He thinks about Whitney: *I mean it's not like we have a firm date or anything. Well, maybe we do.* He thinks dangerously deeper, he regains the positive; *I mean, she did ask me. She asked me straight, if I was coming tonight; I'm here, she's here. So, that's near enough a date, isn't it? Yes it is and I'm for staying the course.*

Confidence restored, he glances back again, but this time no white specs. With a shrug of his shoulders accompanied by a breathy inhalation, Darren makes his move. He's thinking on his feet now. *Thank goodness for the Lynx; no underarm wet-look tonight. But maybe I've gone a bit over-the-top. Oh heck, my armpits, they feel like bird's nests.* His nervous brown eyes continue darting. She's waving. But again he stops and he asks himself; *Ummm, what if she's waving at someone else?* "Nah."

Committed, he returns a self-conscious wave. She however is too engrossed to notice. Undeterred, he swoops. He spurts, "Oh, hi there, Whitney, you, err— you look nice." Her bulbous red lips together with heavy eye make-up and undulating breasts, not to mention a mini skirt covering ... not a lot, knocks his 'chat-up flow' off course. He inhales, and spurts once more, "Did...didn't know you drank, that?" He remains oblivious to the sniggering girls within Whitney's circle.

Undaunted he continues, "Would you like another?" His voice rises in pitch more or less at the speed he is throwing together his ill-thought-out sentences. He hovers, shuffling from foot to foot. He awaits her response. He waits. Finally, she responds.

"Nah no thanks David, I'm fine," was her curt reply. She dismisses him with a 'don't bother me' daggerish stare.

Darren now finds himself out on a limb, on the perimeter. He is demoralized. His earlier confidence dashed. Worse, his inner voice now reports; *she called you David!* He senses that everyone, especially his work mates are laughing at him. Finally, naivety gives way to reality: *It wasn't me she had waved to after all. It must have been to that girl. OMG! She, she's standing beside me, now we're shoulder to shoulder. Help!*

But, before he can pluck up the courage to speak or just nod or even smile, she too has been drawn into Whitney's coven. He sighs; *...not a date after all. Bummer! Same old story – Darren dumped.* As his lonely walk back to the side-lines gathers momentum his thoughts re-engage; he glances back. He catches yet another glimpse of the tall girl with white specs. He thinks; *She, she really is very nice. I wonder?...* A wide smile has broken across Darren's face. He has options...

# The Midnight Hour

The party is in full swing, it's approaching the midnight hour. Darren has adopted a position deep within the crowded bar area. His earlier Whitney rebuttal, nay *his* stupidity in believing that he was on a date, continues to knock him. He gulps another swig of his Coke. An ice cube moment shocks his mind into a modicum of clear thinking; he wonders if it was his workmate's who had hatched the plan, had they 'set him up'? Had Whitney been in on it? Had he been a complete idiot? As his mood deepened he had even wondered if she was the ring leader. *Nah she's not that cruel.* He takes another gulp, burps and decides to call it a night.

Suddenly he is aware of being embraced and a familiar voice is asking, "Dav-e darlin' oh you're all alone here, so you are. Like, what's up babe?" But before he can muster an equally cool answer, she is on his arm. She is hauling a now dazed Darren through the throng towards the dance floor, his glass of Coke abandoned on a conveniently positioned table.

"Come on, babe, dance with me. I love this wee song, so I do."

Being led, dragged, a sweat breaks. He is consumed with foreboding. Okay he knows all the right moves, but – only within the sanctuary of his bedroom. From a nervous, somewhat timid start Darren is quickly moving to the likes of GaGa, Rihanna and Timberlake. His confidence has been restored.

Then the mood changes as the DJ fades up 'The Mavericks' and like a 'Strictly' tsunami the compact dance floor is swamped with 'daddy-dancers' and jivers. Musically Whitney has also found herself adrift. She grabs his tie and winds his head down to her level; he cannot believe what he is hearing. Glancing aloft the effect of the strobe lighting on the ceiling causes him to momentarily close his eyes before uttering, almost in mime. "Thank you, Lord..." But immediately he redirects his focus back to her. Having been caught once already, he seeks confirmation, a commitment of sorts. "S–Sorry Whitney, what did you jus..."

"Oh, Dav-e darling you're so slow, like. Come on, we're goin' out for some air, so we are." He swallows hard and follows in her wake – grinning. He breaks into the Maverick's chorus. She glances back at him while tugging at his arm.

***

The quiet of the mist rolling up dimly lit streets is challenged by the echoing of Whitney's heels clicking out of time on a gum-stained pavement. The sound of muffled nightclub music battles against that of distant sirens. A faulty street light flashes intermittently, its timing also out of sync.

"Right babe," she slurs while wedging his bean-pole frame into a conveniently placed door-way, "So, I missed you on Christmas Eve, so let's have it now — my festive snog." Agog, he hasn't time to think. On tip-toes, her hands have clasped his gangly neck. In a micro moment and with finger-tip precision, she has manoeuvred herself into a position which allows her to swallow his thin lips. Caught by surprise he coughs a nervous cough. Their torsos part, he breathes again — deeply. The taste of vodka, a whiff of *Tayto* cheese-and-onion crisps, topped off with the remnants of cigarette combine to induce another cough. However, before he can draw further breath she pulls him again. This time he appears to have got the hang of it. Even the rasping of her teeth brace doesn't deter him – he's in for a third time!

***

Returning to the party her 'lap-dog' in tow, she rejoins her circle. Darren is sent to the bar for cocktail refills. A not so street-wise 'first timer' finds himself more or less cleaned out financially. Nevertheless he obediently delivers the tray of permeating poisons otherwise disguised as a rainbow coloured selection of cocktails. And yet again he is summarily dismissed! Whitney, not unlike a fully fuelled vampire has commenced her blow-by-blow disgorge of her romantic interlude. Her circle, well most of them, are left in alcohol driven raptures.

An innocent Darren remains poised in the positive. His fixed grin belies the fact that his 'services' are now surplus to requirements. Awkwardly he remains on stand-by awaiting the return of the dancing Whitney and her two turkey-trotting friends. His virgin brain finally digests the fact that it will be a long wait. In retreat however, his eyes momentarily meet again with those of that girl, with the white specs.

# A One Woman Man

Darren suddenly realises who she is. Third floor, accounts office, second desk on the right. He adopts a wide grin, he nods across mouthing, 'Hi there.' She smiles, he blushes. Darren however, is quick to arrest any further impure thoughts. He is now a 'one woman man'. Politely, he smiles back again but quickly turns his head away in search of his beloved as again he reminds himself that he is now the boyfriend of ... the lovely Whitney.

As he patiently awaits the return of Whitney from yet another dance floor outing, the 'countdown' has begun: ten, nine ... three, two, one. On cue the DJ fades up *Auld Lang Sang,* the dance version. The room it seems has been transformed into a drunken orgy of kissy-kissy-hugs and cheek-to-cheek embraces and a few hand-holding sing-along circles.

Then out comes the keys to Darren's babe machine. He dangles them in a showy way believing that *his* girl Whitney will suddenly reappear. Instead, an impatient glance back into the dance floor mêlée finds her sucking the life out of another unsuspecting lad's head. That was the final indignity.

"Fuck this for a party!" Darren quietly slips away to his little red car... mumbling, "HAPPY NEW YEAR TO ME...NOT." No heads turn and no one joins in with his toast.

END

# INCIDENT at TWISTED ELBOW

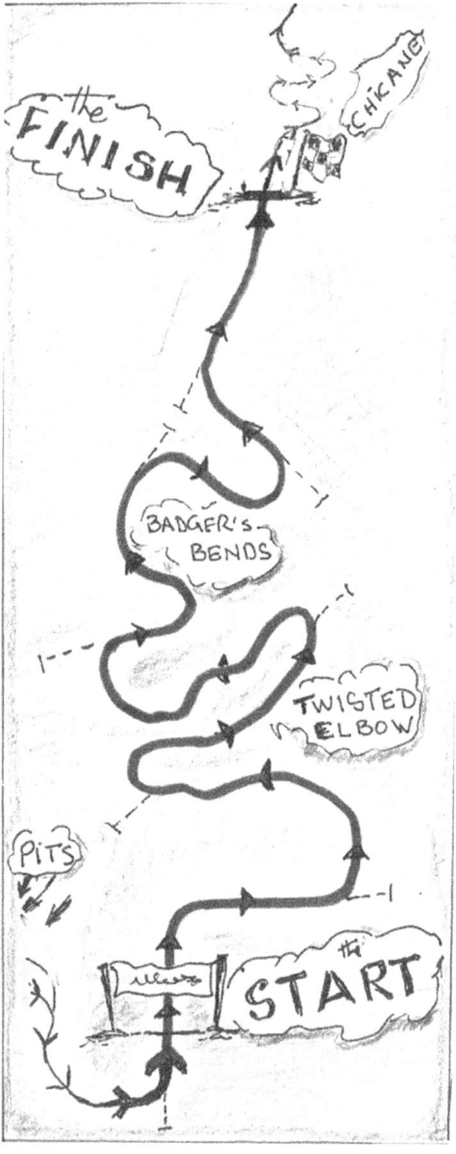

the
FINISH

CHICANE

BADGER'S
BENDS

TWISTED
ELBOW

PITS

the
START

# Meetings

It was an exasperated chairman who was facing an eighteen strong committee split fifty-fifty on a 'one item' agenda. The very thought of using his casting vote had never entered Antony English's mind. He knew of course that he must find a way to resolve the impasse. Okay, he had accepted that a complete conversion to a 'yes' vote would be an unlikely outcome. A workable swing of say, 70% to 30% in favour – his original target – would now require much work and probably several more laborious meetings.

The motion was straight forward enough: A 'yes' vote would allow the Mid County Motor Sports Association (MCMSA) to approve a proposal to reignite the dormant *Twisted Elbow* hill-climb races. A 'no' vote however would not only kill off the proposal but – worst case – probably lead to a general lack of off-road access for other MCMSA events. Antony, known throughout the region as *Tony the Chair* had reached the end of his tether.

However, the back ground rattling of bar shutters conveniently broke the impasse.

"Right folks," said Tony, jumping to his feet, "with the bar open," he paused, "this round's on me. Treat it as a half time break, and another opportunity to see your neighbour's point of view. I'll be back in half an hour where upon we'll recommence, and," he slapped the table, "we'll draw this out to a conclusion, even if it runs into extra time. Gentlemen, ladies we need a result – but the right result."

To say that the *Twisted Elbow* hill-climb event had had a reputation would be something of an understatement. The event had for years provided an annual gift for those with a need for speed. It challenged every driver. Now, some ten years later, it was poised to make a return to the British motorsport calendar, but only if the MCMSA could return a comfortable 'yes' vote.

On his return, Tony the Chair was met with a more agreeable committee. Most had taken advantage of the chairman's generosity, several though had gone home. Those who remained seemed to have undergone something of an epiphany. In fact those remaining members easily approved the proposal, but not as comfortably as Tony would have liked.

In the process of closing the meeting he delegated a somewhat sceptical Honorary Secretary to pass the *good* news onto the Dewhurst family representatives. At the same time his inner voice had summed up, '*A win is a win, even though we've much work to do, going forward! And as for the Dewhurst girl, I just hope it all goes well. It had been a really brave decision for her, the local librarian, to bring forward her family's proposal.*' Tony the Chair among others, had been impressed with her maturity and eloquence when she had delivered her presentation. It was, after all, a hell of a thing she was doing.

***

Reflecting on its success a buoyant but impatient *Dewhurst girl* found herself now tempering her enthusiasm as another day passed with still no official communication from MCMSA.

The said proposal had been made possible in the first instance by the good grace of two local families: Lord MacFinch and the aforementioned Dewhurst's. Access to under-used estate roads or abandoned single tarmac tracks would not only lengthen the original course but offer new challenges for each and every driver.

Still, she and the families awaited a response; the Association's 'yes' was starting to look like retracted 'no'. Frustration had got the better of Danielle Dewhurst. It led her to corner Antony English as he was preparing to chair yet another of his charity meetings. However, it was the blank look on his face which alerted her that skulduggery may well have been afoot within the MCMSA committee.

In something of a stutter he said, "Ah–ah; just you leave that with me Dani... darling."

Alarm bells now rang for Danielle Dewhurst as *her* inner voice advised; *Tread carefully Dani, not everyone at MCMSA is your friend!*

Two days later a letter fell through the Dewhurst letter box...

***

Following the official announcement – the Notice of Racing – word spread fast and if the avalanche of enquires and a plethora of early entries was a barometer of event interest then bad memories of that fateful day, which ended the *Twisted Elbow's* run, had been consigned to history. While this *Twisted Elbow* event wouldn't claim to be the longest or highest hill-climb in the UK – that accolade remained with Larne Motor Club – this new styled outing promised to challenge the whole field right up to that summit.

On the Friday of the event competitors studied the built-in intricacies of the new course while booking practice runs. Marshalls by the dozen set-up camp along the course with ambulance, fire engine and tow-truck stations being prepared for a catalogue of expected thrills ... and more especially, spills.

Hard to imagine this same vista choked in a cocktail of burnt fuel, exhaust fumes and smoking rubber; very much a case of machinery versus nature. Thoughts and visions of the rich topography of hillocks and vales would be well down each personalised racing agenda. Time to enjoy the associated wildlife: birds in song and beasts a-grazing, non-existent too. The tapestry of autumn foliage morphing from greens to a landscape of gold and red would be left to the Saturday and Sunday hoards to absorb ... if the screaming of highly tuned engines allowed.

In its original guise the event had been a one-day twisting incline towards the summit. This time however the event would differ from the usual formats of the various clubs making up the MCMSA's programme. *Twisted Elbow* had been billed as a motorsports weekend spectacular.

The reconfigured course had been enabled by the coming onboard of Lord Sidney MacFinch and his offer to open up several tarmac and concrete estate roads. According to the pre-event blurb, this modified course promises to be not only fast, but endowed with deceivingly perilous bends and dips where disaster lurks for the unprepared or gung-ho driver.

To those who had never forgotten, it seemed to be quite a crass thing to write. Perhaps most people didn't remember the incident which had resulted in a tragic loss of life all those years ago. Not a millimetre of rubber had left its mark on the *elbow* since.

# Partnership

Time was now very much against Messer's Shawcross and Abernethy. The starting line was only a matter of months away and a late season recurring engine issue had left them completely stumped. A drop in their shared car's performances had translated into a dual nemesis which buried deep within their psyche. More importantly, both their personal rankings had been affected.

It seemed like only yesterday when these partners were debating whether the hulk of a wrecked and dis-owned *Mike Pilbeam* race car could be salvaged, rebuilt and crucially be made competitive again. Considered as a re-build project, folk came, looked, prodded and kicked tyres, but ultimately walked away. Young Shaw-cross however had had second thoughts having revisited the aforementioned heap of (scrap) metal and 'single use plastic'. Privately, he felt sure that he could transform this frog back into a princess – he just knew.

In passing he had also unearthed some history of this yellow wreck. It was a unique *Pilbeam MP89 Vrage* and a rare two-seater to boot!

His partner remained unimpressed, but nevertheless kept close to Phil ... just in case. Crucially their current steed, a trusty *Ford Escort special* had been retained in its fully tuned mode, just in case. The owner of the wreck was only too happy to say goodbye to the corpse. Not much money changed hands.

Phillip Shawcross was the mechanical brains of their partnership. The older, taller William Abernethy was at the business end of their team, He was self-titled the cash builder. They were in many way's opposites but their partnership worked, most of the time.

***

The return of *Twisted Elbow* had created a brand new challenge for the Mid County racers. It would be the closing event of hill-climb season. The air of excitement and expectation was building for both driver and organising team. The Shawcross-Abernethy re-build had gone well and their vehicle — referred to as the Lazarus machine — made its debut at one of the early hill climbs the previous year. Phil and Will however found themselves hopelessly out of their depth!

Thereafter, many hours practicing out on a nearby disused airfield followed. As a consequence, both drivers delivered much improved finishes at outing number two of that season. More hours were spent on the *Pilbeam* during the off-season. Now in their second season the performance graphs were charting continued improvement to the point where both of them were seriously chasing silverware and importantly prize money, meagre as it was. The end-of-season event – the *Twisted Elbow* – loomed large.

Still sharing the *Pilbeam*, both boys were confident they could win the race. Curiously it would also be a personal race between the two of them, driving the same car. Will, due to a win at the penultimate event of the season, saw his ranking move three places ahead of Phil's. The race was indeed on, but only if their car's engine issues could be sorted in time. But time was not in their favour.

Admitting defeat in the tracing of the recurring engine problems, both boys agreed that professional assistance was needed, and immediately. Will, of his own volition had set the ball rolling. He had duly presented Phil with an arresting piece of headed notepaper. It had come by way of a favour from one of Will's business contacts who was not only a valued customer but a family friend; his father was an old school pal of Mr. Abernethy Senior. Crucially, he was also the proprietor of a specialist garage renowned in motorsport circles for race-car preparation and especially engine proficiency.

Phil, while concealing his surprise at being presented with such a document, an estimate or quote he wasn't sure, had remained dead-pan. His steely eyes swallowed the prices line by line. He lowered himself to his hunkers and read the document again. Still he remained silent. Finally rising to his full height of five foot six, he ran his fingers through shoulder length hair turned and faced his partner. Almost in a whisper, while slapping the document with the back of a hand, he asked, "Why?"

Before Will could respond Phil continued, his voice rising, "Mate, we're supposed to be partners and in my book partners communicate and make joint decisions, yes?"

Will remained silent.

Staring at the paperwork again, Phil said, "Have, have you agreed to this price? I'm asking, because this may well look to you as our saviour." He paused and again he slapped the document – harder this time, his voice rose by an octave or two, his ample eyebrows scrunched, "But have you thought, just for a moment, that this may seriously compromise me, financially? That, and I'm not kidding, it could force me to quit our partnership. Did you?"

It was a rattled Will who found himself searching for a one liner that would calm his partner down but crucially give him some time to understand why Phil had become so animated. More importantly, Will needed to understand why his mate, his friend, would want to dissolve their long running partnership, nay even their friendship. His mind raced trying to understand what was going on, but all he could think was, 'Jeez, talk about getting something shoved back in your face. So much for good faith and friendship.'

The document he had acquired for them – in good faith – had been slapped onto the fat rear tyres of the *Pilbeam*. It shouted back at the partners. It required action. It was a use-it or lose-it type of option.

In spite of Will's family connections and all the talk of mate's rates, the price which continued to scream inside Phil's head was way above what he had expected. In reality he'd had no real concept of the market rates because it was him, the expert 'spanner man' who kept their old *Ford Escort special* running. This however was much more of a technical beast, complex in the extreme.

The more they interrogated the figures the more the final total bawled at them ... and worse. Phil queried his partner further, "Will, is this an estimate or a quote, which?" He paused, drew breath before continuing his onslaught, "Oh holy shit man, this is a bloody disaster. A disaster that's what it is!"

Squirming, Will tried to soften the reality by suggesting that it might be an estimate, so the final bill could be lower. He stabbed at the bottom line of the document. Facing Phil squarely, he said firmly, "As it stands mate, *this* is the reality."

"Mate, you're grasping at straws. Wise up and engage that business brain of yours. Estimates rarely offer reductions. Hell's teeth William, don't you get it?"

Will responded, his voice rising, "Look Phil, we've been pissing into the wind for far too long. This whole engine carry-on needs sorted." He paused, drawing himself up to his full height, before continuing with his defence. "If you'd listened to me in the first place, well ... we wouldn't be in this fix ... but no." He paused again, taking a breath, trying to calm his emotions, but deciding simply to continue with *his* onslaught, "You had to sort it out yourself, didn't you? To be fair, you nearly did, but listen wee man, you know just as well as I do, that damned hic-up is still there. Not as severe I admit, but it's still there. Let's get it sorted once and for all, and let's for goodness sake get this baby up and purring and let's see if one of us can win that prize money. Come on mate, let's do this, please."

Phil, with head bowed, stood still and silent. He had absorbed enough of Will's lecture. But crucially, even though he wanted to fire back, he had no answer. Deep within he knew the big lad was correct. Inside however, his temper continued to boil. Before he could come up with the words he needed, Will pressed on.

"Phil, look …come on, look at this." He took hold of the estimate, ran his finger down the list of items. A forefinger hovered over the rate that had been quoted or maybe estimated. "For goodness sake Phil, I mean look at that. This chappie, I'm sure, is actually doing this at something near cost price. I know him, know the family. I'd bet you, he won't rip us off. So, come on mate I ask you again … Let's get this frippin' engine up to speed again."

By now Phil had walked away. Squinting, he had walked out into the low sun and lit a cigarette. He needed to clear his head. Once again reality had hit him smack between the eyes. It was of course a no-brainer, no work done on the engine, no *Twisted Elbow*, no winnings, and … the end of the road for them, probably.

Time was against them and finding alternative garages for alternative prices was an unrealistic prospect. The reality was that of a financial *fait accompli* but one which would impact seriously on Phil's meagre savings. In that moment it confirmed for him that the further up the rankings one climbed, the faster finance races ahead of, well, everything!

Sucking the remaining life from his cigarette he edgily returned to the garage. Oozing a noticeable air of defeat, and perhaps self-doubt, he finally agreed that the engine could go off to the experts.

Will was happy, jubilant even. However he quickly realised that it was far from being a win/win scenario.

It was the general lack lustre response from Phil that was most troubling.

Over a much needed coffee and a calmer discourse, Phil managed to explain, without shouting, why he had such misgivings and how badly his savings would be hit. Will, suddenly aghast by his own blindness was immediately apologetic. In his enthusiasm and *his* no-brainer solution, he hadn't considered for a moment the disparity of their disposable income levels.

Their project had been conceived as a 50-50 venture. Along the way Phil was of course aware that Will had from time to time, topped up the car account at the local Halifax bank. He labelled it as additional sponsorship or a wee donation. Although a proud Phil had to ignore these contributions, the reality was that without actual financial partnerships in the form of a sponsor or two, or more, the project would fail now.

Will, as a means of making things right between them – to even things out – had, as Phil suggested, already engaged his business brain. He quietly vowed that the dreaded sponsorship would be found. "Trust me, wee man."

Phil forced a smile, presented his hand for a high five while saying, "I do trust you, honest I do. Honest." And with that they had parted; the big lad off to addresses unknown, the wee lad homeward, for a much needed shower.

***

As he stood there drenched and with soap stinging his tired eyes he worried if whatever moneys raised would ever be enough to cover the engine estimate. By the time he'd dried off, he had agreed with himself that the question would keep for another day.

Theirs had always been a joint campaign; joint in the sense that it saw them sharing one car, but also competing against each other in that same car, and in the same class. Each operated a Direct Debit which paid into a car account at the Halifax. Having to send the engine away had instantaneously stripped that account bare. The *Twisted Elbow* event had therefore taken on a whole new level of importance; a healthy one-off prize fund to be chased.

Sharing one car suited both of them. It had created complications at times. Their height and build differences demanded that the seat and steering wheel be repositioned for every run. It could become a bit of a pantomime at times. They were not the only competitors sharing cars. Most of the motor clubs around the circuit were understanding, and supportive.

***

Bubbling with anticipation, the engine delivery was imminent. An array of associated jobs had been completed on schedule. Phil, whose proper job was as the chief engineer at a nearby garage and coachworks, had taken a week's leave. Will, who was a high-end commercial sales representative, was moving up onto the management ladder. He was very much time poor in a fast expanding business sector.

Added to these pressures, Will was, unlike Phil, no longer single, thus he was always balancing his time between business commitments, motorsport and home life. His big result at the previous event had moved him up towards the top of their class. Phil might have been acknowledged as something of a genius on the 'spanners' but out on the track he had a tendency to overcook the corners. Seconds, it was all about saving seconds. Providing spectacular smoking tyres had made him a spectator favourite, but regularly this ate up valuable time. Will in contrast was a cool customer. He had a natural ability to get the best from his steeds whether it was in their former ex-rally car or now with the *Pilbeam* or lately, in his ... racing sailboat; another addition to his time squeezed portfolio.

Without the luxury of a proper pit crew a high proportion of their leisure time, Phil's certainly, had been consumed on DIY mechanicals. On the motorsport calendar there was little room for other pastimes. However Will's new latest love – sailing – had a tendency to overlap proceedings, especially when the lighter nights approached. It was much to Phil's annoyance. The hangover from their argument about the refurbishment of the engine still lingered. Added to it the time constraints of Will's commitments were bringing things to a head again. The frequency of their big bust-ups was increasing.

Hoisted on jacks within their spacious shed on the Ashbourne Road, their new car (more of a shell) was having its engine mountings replaced in readiness for its re-sorted power source. Time, as always, was not their companion – it was a Sunday evening and the boys had mere days left to make Lazarus arise and be race worthy again!

# Life and Death

Danielle and Daisy Dewhurst were identical twins. They were the giggly teenage daughters of Joe and Mary Dewhurst. The old road ran parallel to one side of their family farm; it had done so since well before the inception of the hill-climb. The event had over the years got nick-named the *Twisted Elbow* after a notorious hairpin section. It had generated a catalogue of car wrecking incidents.

They had grown up with it. Danielle dreaded it. Her sister on the other hand, counted down the days. The noise of the high revving engines, the colour, the spectacle, and of course the talent – Daisy was boy mad.

In looks and stature, with the exception of hair styles, they were virtually indistinguishable. By day, Daisy sported long blond swishy pony tails while her sister did not. Equally, Daisy's dress code seemed to revolve around short shorts and gaping blouses or tight t-shirts. Unlike her sister, Danielle much preferred to dress down. She cultivated the image of a plain Jane. However, in private they were close as only twins could be. This feature had become stronger as they matured. They were approaching sixteen years of age; Danielle was the elder by a handful of minutes. Their older brothers John and James, also twins, were complete opposites. One was of compact build with jet black hair while the other was tall and ginger haired. They were nicknamed accurately, if unimaginatively, Blackie and Ginge. Fashion for them revolved around the latest boiler suit from the men's unisex collection at the local agri-merchants.

Both brothers shared Daisy's interest in the mechanical, especially tractors. Danielle however loved her horses and was a regular competitor on the local Point-to-Point scene. She was good. When away from her equine world she was studying music. To say that she played the violin well would be an exaggeration. Her sister was also a music lover but from a gramophone, very loudly. It was the cause of recurring family discussions...

Brother John had finally completed the restoration of a little classic grey Ferguson tractor. It noticeably gleamed. Daisy had quickly commandeered it – immediately her favourite toy. She never developed a similar relationship with Danielle's horses.

The Dewhursts had, as they always did prior to the event, moved her little equine family away from the hill-climb course. Daisy had been a willing helper but continually she would question her sisters over the top precautions by saying that the animals would love to watch the action. Danielle just shook her head, and smiled. She was not going to respond to her sister's wind-ups.

By late afternoon that year the job was done. It had been particularly strenuous. Neither of the brothers had been available and the exercise had been made worse by an early fading light abetted by angry clouds, sleet and a biting wind. Finally, and with a feeling of achievement Daisy revved up the classic tractor in triumph. The rattle of the elderly engine and the vertical exhaust of grey smoke signalled the end of activities.

With urgency, and in spite of John's lecturing on why the elderly tractor should be treated kindly, Daisy had rammed it into gear and accelerated so hard that the front wheels pointed skywards!

Having exited the field, and with mud being spun heavenwards Daisy accelerated the tractor up through the gears. They fairly tore up the well-worn tarmac side-road that more resembled a track with its central strip of grass.

With yelps and hollering, Danielle hung on while standing behind her sister and singing along to the transistor radio. It was stuck to the dashboard with duct tape. Full volume was needed to compete with noise of the engine. Her sister had the tractor wound up to near full throttle ... no notion of her brother's pep-talks had entered her head.

Both girls were looking forward to baths, food and for later on, the motor club's pre-event party at the nearby pub. This would be first year that they would not be chaperoned.

Daisy was in a joyous mood. The weekend held the prospect of another exciting festival of fast cars and smoking tyres as well as meeting up with Phil Shaw-cross. She had a crush on him. They had first met at a similar event some season's previously.

There had been an immediate attraction; good looks and matching long hair. He was older, she was taller. It was a teenage romance which never really got going. His head, she soon discovered, continually buried itself under bonnets. Dating revolved around his race scene, a backseat and her homework – but she really fancied him. Her sister couldn't understand the attraction; all far too juvenile for her.

The warmth of the farmhouse, and those hot baths beckoned — just a final dash across the junction ahead. Only a few hundred yards. The time they had saved by Daisy gunning the engine had been precious.

***

Whether the brakes on the ancient tractor were wet and clogged in mud or just weren't working properly had been unclear. A competitor had been using that Friday afternoon for an unscheduled practice. It was a practice opportunity very much frowned upon by on the organisers.

The inquest returned a verdict of misadventure, the rogue driver was prosecuted.

Daisy had held onto life for approximately a week and a half, but her head and crush injuries proved too severe. Her sister survived the impact with cuts, bruises, and a broken arm. That year's hill climb was abruptly cancelled. And since that fateful Friday the seasonal venue had remained dormant. Many years of silence had passed...

***

For the Dewhurst family time had never come close to healing the pain of losing Daisy. Life on the farm however maintained its required pace. The constant challenge of using the cross-roads where the accident had occurred was constant. It was the farm's linkage, the crossing point between their fields – and a daily reminder.

Danielle's horses had gone to new owners. The endless sadness, the continual mourning and the premature aging of her parents had become too much to bear. She knew that something had to be done to lift the overbearing family gloom while maintaining an air of respect for her sister, and family.

With her parents attending a church function and with her brothers securely seated around the family sized mahogany dining table she had plucked up the courage to unwrap her long-thought-out, and until that point, secret proposal.

Her opening thoughts were to present the key elements of her proposal to James and John in bullet format thus teasing out any major negatives before delivering the full document. It had been a late night. Satisfied, she would deliver it to their parents the following weekend, perhaps after Sunday lunch and maybe in an abridged format as well; maybe not? Danielle spent the following week locked in her room putting together the agreed amendments.

Her parents, not surprisingly, displayed little in the way of enthusiasm for her proposal, regardless of whether or not it was in the memory of her motor sport mad sister.

Both brothers had supported her and eventually Joe and Mary's reluctance had lessened. While their full support was not forthcoming, they nevertheless did not outwardly display negativity; theirs became a neutral stance. With a degree of understatement Danielle had transmitted her proposal to Tony the Chair and with his support she copied it to the MCMSA secretary for discussion at the soonest opportunity. Their AGM.

At the appropriate juncture of the meeting, the incoming committee's first business was to formally receive the Dewhurst proposal. Danielle, accompanied by her brother John, duly delivered her presentation and accompanying documentation. The siblings were confident that they would receive the new committee's immediate support. She was ecstatic. On the one hand, buoyed at her own business-like drafting of the said proposal and on the other, by leading the family in a lasting memorial to her beloved late sister. However, the support was not immediate and so, she went into waiting mode.

Having presented the proposal, she and her brother treated themselves to a celebratory drink at the downstairs bar. It was then that her eyes met those of Phil Shawcross. They'd not seen each other or spoke since the funeral those many years past. Contact had been completely lost. Now though, the conversation between the three of them was polite, and despite the gap of time, not strained at all. She found him to be an entirely different person to the daft long-haired eejit that her sister had found so fanciable. It fact he was now a mature, handsome young man.

During the days that followed the chance encounter, Danielle found herself in something of a quandary. She was unsure why she had accepted his nervously issued dinner invitation. He was, or had been, her dead sister's boyfriend. Yet it had all seemed so natural; a catalyst which in turn created something of a dining out (dating) embryo. As time progressed she discovered they shared numerous likes, and yes, some dislikes. Yet a relationship of sorts had taken root. It grew in spite of her abhorrence of motor sport.

***

Phil was secreted within a vacant engine compartment, his position almost acrobatic as he rotated a spanner to tighten an awkwardly positioned engine mounting nut. Body deranged his head and shoulders obscured. Only his plumber's bum and splayed legs were visible from outside. Will, who had arrived directly from yet another client meeting retained his usual cool self; donning his white, barely stained overalls, he remained deaf to his partner's snide banter. With hands gloved in blue latex, he held the bracket.

He was leaning over Phil in such a way that if photographed their position would require some discreet explanation. During the process of intimate conversation — their heads almost face-to-face — Phil uncharacteristically and without fanfare, suddenly confided, "Listen mate," he paused. An air of hesitation had washed over him. Will's curiosity level rose. Phil summoned his strength. "I'm in a bit of a quandary. I, um..." He stopped. He had restarted his extraction from the depths of the engine compartment. Will did the same; the manoeuvre could have been titled, Operation Octopus.

"Right, come on wee lad. Spit it out. Tell your older, wiser, taller chum your symptoms. It's that Danielle, you've got her pregnant." Will was on top form, enjoying the intrigue and seeing his wee mate squirm.

"Chance would be a fine thing."

Will resisted further teasing, and merely waited.

"Yeah, you're right, as bloody usual. It's about 'Dani. Look mate, she's inside my head. Friggin heck I don't know how to take this forward. I mean, I want to. I um, like— I fancy her to bits. But it's not right—I mean—she's Daisy's sister for fuck's sake! Do you understand? And as well, what have we really got in common: horses, cars, cars and horses? Not a great combination?" Now down on his hunkers and leaning against the offside front wheel, his hands tightly knotted, he asked, "Why is life so friggin' complicated?"

After a short tumble weed of silence, Will replied, "Not being an expert in such matters, you're asking me..." Silence reigned until Will resumed, "Em…fancy a pint?"

"Yes, indeed I do big lad. Just give me a moment to clean up."

As well as Phil's matters of the heart the intensity of the work-load that they had set themselves had been lifted, albeit slightly. The notion of a pint had been an inspirational suggestion. It had been a while since they'd had some boys' time out together.

Although they only downed a couple of lagers each it had been a late session; a deep session during which both of them came to realise that their whole motor sport obsession was using up far too much of their leisure time. Issues such as Phil's Dani dilemma had been allowed to fester. Just being able to mention it out loud allowed his brain – the bit that looked after romance and stuff – to generate its own answers. Leaving the pub that night Phil knew, there and then, what his next course of action towards Danielle should be.

*I'll keep my plan under wraps until I've pocketed the prize-winning cheque and am the first name inscribed on the new Dewhurst Cup.*

# Hill Climb - Saturday

The MCMSA Motor Sport Spectacular weekend had arrived. Phil and Will's engine was purring and the costs in relation to the contentious paperwork had come in at well under what had been quoted, or estimated. It didn't matter which it had been now. A smug Will passed the paperwork to Phil saying quietly, "That'll do for me."

Phil said nothing.

The remnants of an early morning downpour had cleared and this long awaited race day was brightening at pace. Thus, prospects of a perfect autumn event remained in the positive. The majority of the team at MCMSA had been on site from the early hours. Roads and dedicated parking areas were clogging up: tents, gazeboes, makeshift canopies and picnic rugs littered the roadside fields. Spectators clambered for space and for the best viewing spots. Expectation filled the chill air. The safety car continued to patrol the route, its onboard tannoy booming busy encouragement for stragglers to deposit themselves.

The organisers had been caught flat-footed though. An early risk assessment suggested that the entire event may have to be abandoned; too many people! Conversations back-stage had become lively. The old guard of naysayers offering useless comments such as, "Never like this when we were in charge – young un's couldn't organise a... And as for all that new-fangled computer stuff? 'elf 'n' safety gone bloody mad!"

A compromise pointed towards delaying the start of the programme. A frustrated Clerk-of-the-Course, driving a liveried *Audi Quattro* complete with a full array of blazing rally spotlights, was revving and ready to do a final sweep of the course. But to no avail. The new start time for the opening race would be twelve noon. The programme would be an hour and a half behind schedule.

This, the organisers figured, would allow both the army of marshalling volunteers the time to fully clear the course of people and complete all the races in daylight. It would be tight. Competitor's frustrations from within and around the starting zone remained loud and clear. The pressure was on. Finally, at 11:45 exactly, the Quattro was fired up. With four smoking tyres it was released... Expectations had finally matured into reality. Roars of horsepower, hot engine oil, torque and smoking rubber drifted from the pits allowing the freshening breeze to carry this performance cocktail across the fields and onto the course itself.

***

Danielle was far across the fields walking and recalling the times when she had tended to her horses. There had, for a number of years been no horses in her life, but like wanting to get the hill climb reconvened, so she had decided to reembrace that most important aspect of her life. A pony and a donkey had come back to live in the fields. She shook her head in disapproval as big gurgling exhausts resonated loudly. However her disapproval was tempered as she reminded herself that it was she who had created the space which allowed the event to be re-run in the first place.

She smiled as memories of Daisy flashed before her eyes. *Oh, that car crazy girl — boy mad.* She was comfortable with her decision as she visualised her late sister straddling a fence cheering on each competitor, especially the unfortunates who failed to negotiate whatever bend that had claimed them.

Daisy's favourite view point had been down by the notorious section nick-named *Twisted Elbow*. Mentally Danielle was okay except when anxious thoughts invaded her head. One in particular had remained stubborn; *What if Phil is the winning driver? Goodness, I'd be handing over the cup to ... my boyfriend. Cheesy?* A fixed grin lightened her thoughts.

***

There was an element of the showman about the Clerk-of-the-Course; he was Hannu Mikkola for the day. His drive was also a check that the roads, the new inclusions especially, were indeed fit for purpose. With mere inches to spare, he swept the big Quattro past roadside hedges and banks. Tyres smoked while its engine screamed between the gears. The educated among the large crowd cheered and inhaled on the building excitement. Prime viewing locations had been filled to capacity. Cameras were made at the ready. Back down at the starting zone twelve noon had struck. Stopwatches were clicked and the newly convened *Twisted Elbow* hill-climb roared back into life.

The most powerful of machinery, group one, were away first: ex-racing and rally cars, specials and the like. There after came the various classes, right down to the novices. Overall, 61 cars would answer the starter's call.

Although they considered themselves still very much as amateurs, both Phil and Will had risen steadily through the ranks. They now found themselves in the ultra-competitive group. Each fancied himself as the class winner. Both had their eye on the prize money! But there were some fancy and formidable cars in their class and excellent drivers too: several *Porches*, a *Lotus Cortina special,* a brace of *Quattro's* plus several *Lotus Super 7's.* Then came the out and out race cars: *Lotus*

*GTUs,* several cars from the *Crosslé company* as well as various *March* models and *Pilbeams,* five of them in total, including their own.

After the warming of tyres in a specially created paddock, Will was the third car away; competitors took off at timed intervals. After his first run, Lazarus, their liveried yellow *Pilbeam* led the class. Finally it was Phil's turn. He was the last driver to go; a technical hic-up concerning his bespoke seat attachment had delayed the transfer of their car from Will's to Phil's seat set-up. It had upset Phil, a mini tantrum the evidence. Will calmed him down, reporting that she was going like a sewing machine. A different car! "Just keep her between the hedges wee man, and watch out for the kink in Badger's Bend."

Badger's bend was a left-hander which immediately followed the infamous hairpin from which the event had derived its name. The course was already living up to its reputation. The officials' concerns were mounting. As well as Danielle's two brothers, various neighbouring farmers and auto repair outfits had their tractors and tele-handlers on standby. They were soon part of the action.

Phil's blood pressure continued to rise as he moved towards the start line. Heart thumping, only a single car sat in front of him. Then finally, and with his engine revs rising, his turn had come. The official – known to all as three-fingers-Freddie – held out his hand. Phil, with both feet working overtime to hold back his steed, had turned the revs up another notch. The official continued his visual countdown: 3 -2 – 1–

A cloud of tyre smoke left no one in any doubt that Phil was on fire in this his first climb of the day. However, as he crossed the finish it was clear that his manor of driving had again proved to be more spectator friendly than a race winning drive. His navigation of the hairpin was sloppy; he'd piled into the notorious section too fast. Expertly though, he'd got away with it albeit, time costly. Next, he blasted through Badger's Bend reclaiming some of his lost time. His fourth place considering his *Elbow* calamity was nevertheless a solid start to his weekend's challenge.

It was now mid-afternoon and the daylight was closing in. Phil was moving up the queue ready for his second run. His concentration however, was drifting; *had Danielle been tempted to take a sneaky look down the course. No chance.* He remembered that she and her mother had planned a shopping outing. He would meet up with her later in the pub at the post-race function. His inner voice interjected – it commanded that he engage his racing brain, and immediately. A shake of his head had quickly cleared the fog. *Sorry girl, got work to do here.* Catapulted back into the here-and-now the engine noise focused him as did three fingers Freddie, 3-2-1-

Even though he had been sluggish off the line this second run had been good for Phil – not so for Will. He had over cooked another of the new bends but with his excellent first run he still held the overall lead, just. Phil's improved time had moved him up to second overall in class. Tomorrow, they agreed, would be another day. Both were glad to have completed their runs in reasonable light. Having loaded their *Pilbeam* expertly into its bespoke colour coded tandem axel trailer, it was with a smile and a high-five they went their separate ways to prepare for later. They had managed to get their runs in just in time. Heavy clouds and hailstones forced the organisers to call a halt to proceedings before the final classes had completed.

***

The phone lines were busy that Saturday evening as the MCMSA officials attempted to inform all the competitors of the necessary programme changes. Communication lines were red hot... Phil's mobile phone had also been busy, but for other reasons.

The text read:

> Listen up wee man - change of plan! My husband is insisting on showing off his professional cheffing skills by cooking a celebration meal tonight. You and Danielle are cordially invited – say 7.30 (ish). OK?

Phil was relieved but Danielle was somewhat averse. Nevertheless she agreed to go. Anything she thought, would be better that listening to a pub full of inebriated petrol-heads droning on about, well everything she detested. Phil, unbeknown to her had similar misgivings. But his were more to do with his reservations about high-end dining, he being more of an all-day-fry or Big Mac man.

As they made their way to Will's place both shared their general concerns, but also agreed that it had to be a better option than merely getting pissed and, for sure, for him having to compete with a brain bursting hangover the following day.

Both smiled while the doorbell chimed it's over-the-top tune. Introductions were made as Will's husband, Geoffrey, presented everyone with his special welcoming aperitif – a chilled white port. Phil and Danielle's contribution of an expensive (for them) Malbec bought en route seemed somewhat paltry. Small talk ensued and as Danielle had suspected, her boy and his big mate soon became embroiled in 'auto-talk'.

Geoffrey however had morphed into the chef-cum-master of ceremonies. Danielle and he listened patiently to the boys' daring deeds of the day. That was until he expertly moved his and Danielle's conversations smoothly away and into the finer things of life.

Recipes, decor, fashion, the equine world, anything really, other than that which reeked of petrol. The evening had flown. Thanks mostly to the wine and Geoffrey's excellent hosting skills, which had effectively droned out the auto-talk.

It was however to be an early evening exit. The two boy-racer's energy levels were low and by 10:45 p.m. Phil and Danielle were sedately driving back towards her farm house in his father's big gleaming Volvo estate car. Danielle was still bathing in a fine dining and alcohol drenched evening of luxury. As well as the food she had enjoyed Geoffrey's wine master class and his never ending tales.

Easing her seatbelt, she leaned across the expansive centre consul and while gently squeezing Phil's thigh, said, "An excellent night, Mister Phil Shawcross. I just loved it, and that Geoffrey boy, what a character?"

Phil smiled. She kissed his neck, asking, "Why didn't you warn me?"

Phil laughed as he always visualised Will as Geoffrey's bit of rough.

"What's funny?"

His answer was dismissive; an attempt he recognised as a way to try to disguise his mild discomfort with homosexuality. "Oh, nothing, Dani, nothing at all my lovely."

She looked at him with a sternness but fell for his fixed grin. Leaning across the console again, this time she didn't pull back as their passion built. Without a single moment more of hesitation, she let her desire drive her.

As she reclined into the passenger seat and he squirmed his way back behind the steering wheel, the dashboard clock came into focus. It had gone one o clock! A frantic re-buttoning and zipping saw them enjoying a final passionate kiss before a somewhat dizzy. but smiling Danielle, was deposited at the farm house door.

# Hill Climb - Sunday

Sunday morning at *Twisted Elbow* had been a busy affair. The organiser's attempts to buy back time and bring the event onto schedule had mixed success. While the entry list which had outstripped even the most generous of forecasts was great for the coffers it had thrown up a whole raft of logistical issues; not least, completing the event in daylight.

A modified programme, announced the previous evening at the post-race social, proved unpopular. Sunday morning practice sessions had been cancelled in favour of re-running the last two classes of the previous day; the novices. Their racing, abandoned late on Saturday evening due to the unseasonal burst of hailstones, was to be the first event on the Sunday.

The programme got underway sharp at 9:30 but another crash brought out the red flags; it was becoming a crisis. The *Twisted Elbow* itself had been the contributor to the delays. Its hairpin bends came at the end of a fast straight on the old course and lay in wait under the edge of an outcrop of mature trees. Long branches created a ceiling under which the camber of the road had long since developed into a fall ... the wrong way. An ancient stone wall was the protector against a steep descent into a deep gully waterfall and stream. It was no friend to bodywork!

Will's first run at 10:15 was clean and safe but his second had been disastrous. He stuttered on the starting line then uncharacteristically spun Lazarus off the flat concrete section of Lord MacFinch's estate. Even worse, his lead was lost to one of the other *Pilbeams* which had been snapping at both Will and Phil all weekend. With one bad run, his grasp for the cash was gone! But it was an inspired Phil who moved into a challenging position.

With the course dried out the pendulum had swung in favour of the afternoon drivers and fat slick tyres. With the field slimmed down – many competitors were only doing the Saturday climbs, while the tail-end of most of the classes had already packed up – this would be the final run of the whole event. All eyes were focused on Phil. He knew what he had to do, he looked at the clear sky, he slapped his palms on either side of his purple racing helmet then onto the wheel. He knew that only the fastest time of the whole weekend would win the money! The yellow car had never felt so good and more importantly, Phil was comfortable with the idiosyncrasies of the course, wet or dry.

As the rising engine revs screamed for release and the crowd, pressing on all sides, roared on their approval and encouragement, Phil's world fell silent. He focussed on his fingers wrapped around the wheel. He stared down the track, he saw the edges of his vision blur and the centre come into sharp relief. The black of the road, the straight down to the first corner. He saw in his mind every turn, every angle, every gear change and braking point. His whole being seemed to merge with the car that thrilled under his touch. In a detached corner of his mind he recognised that he was in the zone. He was ready. The official positioned himself by the driver's side window, his arm was outstretched. 3–2–1–

# Memories

Danielle awoke with a jerk. Smiling, she had a devilish feeling of guilt. Her thoughts swirled in a whirl; *Oh my goodness what came over me last night...? Well— well— well, missy, you've really done it now! Poor Phil wasn't expecting that! Your poor boy never knew what hit him.*

Danielle Dewhurst, in that same moment, found herself being catapulted back into reality. The metallic sounds from the hill-climb had broken through a lightly opened sash window. She switched on the bed-side radio and turned up the volume. She drifted back into a slumber, she was no night-bird. Suddenly she sat bolt upright.

"Agh! Look at the time." Leaping out of bed she grabbed her gown and flew towards the bathroom. *I'll get breakfast later. Goodness, look at the time. Oh my poor babies – I'm coming, I'm coming my equine lovelies.* Recently a new pony named, Nell and a rescue donkey had been re-stabled on the farm and now she needed to get to those stables. The poor animals wouldn't be getting breakfast without her.

***

Frustration consumed her. She was being held back from dashing across the road into her field, despite pleading  with the Marshall. She knew that she could be across and over the galvanised gate opposite in a couple of strides. Her impatience could not be hidden as she stamped from foot to foot. Cold stares targeted the pompous Marshall. "Oh for Goodness sake, John I need to get to Nell and the donkey."

"Calm down sis; I sorted them earlier." With a chuckle he continued, "Wee bit of a late night, eh?" Her brother looked quite professional in his marshal's attire, but she wasn't going to tell him that. "Lover boy's going well this morning. Want to hang around and watch?"

In an attempt to conceal her embarrassment she spun away from him saying; "No chance, bloody cars and boy-racers, I've got better things to do today. Last thing I need is to be stuck here until the flippin' prize giving, and the giving away of our cup, then enduring those awful speeches. Agh!"

"Yeah, whatever, Sis. You're the reason this is all happening," John said and gave her a wide grin.

She rolled her eyes, but content that her 'babies' had indeed been attended to she returned to the homestead. Most Sundays for her and her mother were graveyard visiting days. She had no intention of disturbing their routine although she was privately tempted to hang around—just in case Phil...

But as she strolled back up the lane an uneasiness fell about her that she couldn't put into words or even tangible thoughts. There remained huge empathy for her sister but this was different. With her kitchen door in view, her thoughts cleared. there and then it all made sense. As she shuffled along, pinging the wire between fence posts, she realised that it was all about this event and everything that surrounded it. Had it and her big plan of getting it reconvened, generated an undertone of family stress? She recalled recent arguments between her brothers. She realised her father had become even more withdrawn. It was, she knew, his way of coping with reality. Although he had always put on a brave face, time was no healer in his case. Losing *his* Daisy in such tragic circumstances had altered his entire personality, stooping him in spirit and body. Coming out of his frequently occurring mood swings he could often be heard to mumble, "Never thought I'd bury my own children." Her mother in many ways was handling the atmosphere best. But again Danielle knew not to scratch too deeply as she too was living a life behind welled up eyes.

Taking slower and slower steps, kicking tufts of grass and weeds poking up through cracks in the concrete lane she wondered whether this whole hill-climb reawakening had been such a great idea after all. Okay, she had finally conceded that the record entry and the general turnout was testament to the esteem in which her sister, and indeed the whole family were held. But by the time she reached the kitchen, tears were flooding down her cheeks. Father was first to see her. Moving assertively he hugged his daughter, it was clumsy but it was compassionate. He knew exactly why she was in the state she was.

He said quietly, "Danielle, listen to me. Don't you dare feel any guilt for bringing this back to our front door. It's been good for the community and it's good for the family. It's allowed us all to remember..." he paused, squeezed his nose with a gnarled thumb and forefinger, he coughed and continued, "...to remember what was great about your sister. Sure, she'll be sitting on a fence down there counting the cars through. She'll be in her element, on top form." Danielle kissed his cheek and wiped a runaway tear.

Her mother entered the kitchen and sensing the emotion in her daughter, insisted she eat what was now more a brunch than a breakfast. By two o'clock, all three of them had piled into the family *Land Cruiser* and following the back lanes they headed for the parish church. It was only a field or two away to the east of the farm but the road closures had made it into a lengthy drive.

# Climax

Phil had fairly fired the yellow *Pilbeam* along the course. Though the helmet visor his eyes mapped the road ahead. He was focused. Inside he was smiling, but also concentrating to gain the precious seconds necessary to renew their bank balance while blanking out the pleasant memories of the previous evening. The last thing he could afford, literally, was a distraction.

Through the first sector the consul-mounted stop-watch indicated he was already seconds to the better on the current winning time. He warned himself about being too cocky; *Hedges, keep her between them. Is she out there secretly cheering me on?* Through sector two, the yellow car was flying. Phil was sure that he had taken the lead. "Hedges! Keep her smooth, listen to the revs, Phil" he said aloud as he changed gear again. He had the *Pilbeam* setup immaculately for the incoming bend., "That's it, lovely." His voice level was increasing .

"Where's the apex— GOT IT!" Then in a micro moment, he thought, *Dani will be impressed – I might even get promoted above those bloody animals. Aye right?* "Woops, watch it son. COME ON, CONCENTRATE PHIL!" he shouted at himself. He was safely through the third sector.

His time was better. He knew he was leading. But he also knew that none of it counted until the finish line. As he entered the fourth, and final sector he started to drive strategically. But he knew that it could be a risky plan. Just as his gung-ho style of driving had lost him precious seconds in previous runs, would being a touch more cautious cost him? Of course he was professional enough to realise that taking his foot off the throttle – cruising – could allow his concentration to wander even more. It was at that precise moment he felt the vibration under him. "What the..."

Thoughts of Dani in the front seat of the Volvo flashed into his mind. He put his foot down to force his concentration back onto the road. Danielle's homestead was fast approaching, and with it, the infamous cross roads. The finish line was within touching distance, he was flat-out, drifting through a comparably slow bend. He had this wrapped up. Spectators were in awe of the young driver as cheers and applause followed in his all-conquering wake. Then, a shockwave of gasps...

*** 

The stillness of the graveyard, located high on the hillside, had been overcome by the distant drone of the hill-climb. Despite her father's hugs and her mother's food, Danielle had remained in her weepy state. Tidying flowers and shrubs around her sister's headstone, she whispered; "Oh sister dear, you and your fast cars." But as she started to rise to her feet a chill and fainting sensation consumed her. Her father grasped her arm, taking her weight, steadying her.

"What's wrong, pet, you look as if someone's walked over your—" he stopped, realising what he had almost said.

Her mother interjected, "Oh good God pet, you're as white as a sheet!"

"No I'm okay Daddy, Mum, just a shiver, and standing up too quickly; I'm okay, honestly..." she said but in her head she thought, *I'm not, something's wrong.*

Far in the distance the unmistakable sound of a crashing car carried in the gentle breeze. As it washed over them they froze to the spot. Simultaneously the three of them spoke in a gasped tone, "Phil—NO!"

***

The journey home was made in quiet riposte. The day's late sun had all but dipped and a sharp chill had invaded what had been snug clothing. There was little in the way of improvement within the vehicle. Dani's father expected to be lambasted again for failing to have the vehicle's heater fixed, but no one spoke. None of the three had a mobile phone on them. No point, no signal up in the hills, and so all they could do was drive and hope. They pulled their clothing tight. No amount of small-talk would have warmed the atmosphere.

The rear lane to their home was closed, so a further diversion via another field was navigated. In the approaching dusk the continuous flashing of blue, red and orange lights was dramatic and  unnerving – too close to home. The not knowing was distressing. For the Dewhurst's it was especially so. The resurrection of every detail, every heartbreak of when they had lost Daisy all those years ago. As they pulled out of the field and up to the back door they were greeted by John and James. Stern-faced, they explained what had happened.

Their sister collapsed.

# Déjà Vu

Thirty days later, as a shower of hailstones rattled the hospital windows, Phil Shawcross started to wake from his coma. Grabbing his hand Dani leapt from the bedside chair that she had commandeered throughout the past month. Tears gushed as she spoke. "Oh Phil you're back, you're finally back. Come on babe come back to me. NURSE— n-u-r-s-e!"

***

Through blurred vision the first outline for Phil was that of Danielle. It was a tear drenched moment made awkward by the jungle of wires, catheters and drips.

As Dani eased herself back on to the bedside chair his welled up line of periphery vision homed in on what appeared to be a silver cup. Phil had no idea why it was stood on his bedside cabinet. Equally, he had no clue as to why he was stretched out on a hospital bed. He was however very much aware that every orifice-bound tube was the cause of his gagging, never mind the frequent spasms of pain raking his body.

"Nurse!" Danielle called out again and at the same instant the full nursing team descended on the small room.

Standing back to allow the medics space, Danielle found herself in a state of confusion, panic even. That turned to shock as Phil suddenly fell back onto the pillow. He was shaking, writhing and thrashing about on the bed. It seemed like an eternity but the medical team had the situation quickly under control. One of the nursing team sensing Danielle's distress comforted her by explaining what had happened and how things looked much worse than they were. All was well..

As Phil Shawcross slipped back into sleep rather than a coma, his parents, Freddy and Myrtle hugged his distressed girlfriend. Quietly the three of them took their seats. Dani squeezed Phil's hand. They maintained their vigil.

Under the renewed calmness of the room the next callers were Will and Geoffrey, hand in hand. They had both been shaken deeply by Phil's dice with death and inspired by his remarkable survival and now, what looked increasingly like his recovery. As Phil slept, Susi, the attending nurse broke up the party and instructed Dani to go home, saying. "He'll still be here in the morning pet. You really need to get your sleep in while you can. You're going to be busy for the next few days." With a soft embrace the nurse directed Danielle and the rest of the visitors to the door.

Whisking her away she said, almost in a whisper that maybe Will and his partner should leave too. "Phil needs his rest so, but thanks for coming guys. Come back soon.". More hugs followed before the lights dimmed over the Shawcross bed.

As the days passed, and Phil stayed awake for longer periods, he continued to have little memory of the crash, other than a certainty that there had been a vibration under his seat as he roared out of Badger's Bend. When Will and Geoffrey were next there, he told them what he recalled.

***

In the absence of a delayed forensic report on the tangled heap of metal which had once resembled a race car and was now nothing more than a pile of metal and fibre-glass, no one: marshals, spectators, competitors, Will, John or James could understand why Phil had swerved so dramatically on his all-conquering run to the finish. It was almost as if he was trying to avoid something, a dog, a deer, a bird perhaps? Something? Someone...?

Shock had telegraphed back down the course that autumn afternoon. Many opinions were offered, some shared but mostly there was a silent inhaling of the awfulness, the tragic conclusion of what was supposed to be a competitive drive within a beautiful country side and a celebration of a new event being added to the mid county motor-sport calendar.

Those that had been closest to the crossroads repeated what they had seen in conversation after conversation. Unusually for such a tale, the details hadn't been glorified or exaggerated. There was no need. It had been seen by so many and the fact needed no fictional enhancements. With the finish in sight Phil's car swerved at full speed, ninety degrees into a firm dirt bank, ricocheted off and spun 720 degrees before launching skyward and barrel rolling along the tarmac road, crossing the finish line upside-down. However this was not the end of the Shawcross hill climb.

As officials dived for cover and spectators gaped at the unfolding drama the car's momentum ploughed it on towards a chicane of hay bales –specifically designed to kill the speed of all cars post finish. As a safety measure it was precautionary and had been effective throughout the weekend but never more so than now. The *Pilbeam* car almost cleared the lot, but by good luck or divine providence, the tallest of the hay had caught him. Phil was dragged from the cockpit unconscious, but alive. Just. To add to the unfolding crisis, the wreckage burst into flames. Several of those assisting suffered burns, but not the driver.

After the emergency services had departed from the scene and whilst Phil was being whisked to the emergency ward of the local hospital, Tony the Chair and the rest of the officiating committee deemed that Phil Shawcross had indeed crossed the finish line and in a time which ironically had crowned him, 'King of the Hill' and the first winner of the Dewhurst Cup.

There were no formal speeches or presentations. The majority of the competitors had quietly packed up. Others like the volunteer officials, the macabre element of spectators and those who themselves were in shock, had gathered in the local pub where it was announced that his Lordship would be making an appropriate address. The morbid atmosphere and an aura of disbelieving déjà vu had washed over everyone. Someone said it resembled a wake awaiting the arrival of a corpse. In the snug, where the full committee had gathered the hushed atmosphere was broken by MCMSA's Hon. Secretary uttering – too loudly – one of her infamous snide remarks, "Aye, from rust to rust and from dust to dust goes the *Twisted Elbow*. We at least live in hope it has finally buried itself."

With scowls, Tony the Chair and his Lordship quickly scurried her out of the pub.

***

Phil Shawcross spent a further five months in hospital, moving from ICU to general wards, with more and more frequent visits to the physiotherapy department. As his fitness levels and muscle building improved, his growing mobility and sheer determination impressed. He had been driven, but was not necessarily in a rush to get back into a cockpit, but to carry out the promise he made to himself that night many months ago as he and Will exited the pub.

Danielle had returned to her duties at the town library. The Dewhurst family had resumed the farm's management – John and James never ceased. Phil's parents reverted to a slower visiting routine. This whole palaver had been tough on them. Then an unexpected day-time visit by Danielle knocked Phil completely off balance.

During that week his mind was not entirely focused on the physiotherapy sessions. Instead it was a little maroon coloured box secreted away in the top drawer of his otherwise empty bedside cabinet which currently drove him. As he was to be discharged in a few days he was using his down time to memorise his proposal. He had even been practicing getting down on one knee! All the medical team and especially the tea lady had been sworn to secrecy.

Following the obligatory welcoming hugs and kisses Danielle pressed her hand onto Phil's chest. Softly she directed him back onto the blue leatherette bedside arm chair. Nervously, she said, "Phil, darling Phil, my superstar..."

He tried to interrupt. "I've so—"

Putting a finger to his lips, she continued, "No, listen to me. Me first! This is really important it will affect both of us. Do you hear me Phil?"

Sensing that there could be a 'Dear John' scenario developing, Phil dropped back into the chair. *Oh no, don't do this to me Dani.*

All that Phil picked out of Danielle Dewhurst's announcement was, ".... THREE MONTHS..." Inside his whole body had turned to jelly! He looked at her in amazement. "Really?"

"Yes, Phil darling, yes. I am three months pregnant. With a tremor in her voice she asked him, "What the hell am I – we – going to do now?

Recovering from his shock, Phil stood up and embraced Danielle. The hug lasted for a tearful eternity. He finally eased himself away. Sitting down on the bed he laid back and reached over to the cabinet. As he opened the drawer he finally said, "Close your eyes please pet, just for a moment."

She obliged. A very quiet but ironically expectant mob of nurses had gathered at the ward's threshold.

With the tiny box welded in Phil's palm he straightened himself but lost balance. He slipped off the edge of the bed landing in a clump by the chair.

"Oh Phil what are you doing to yourself, are you hurt?" asked a spooked Danielle as she tried to lift him back up onto the bed. He however was determined to remain on the floor.

"No, no, I'm dead on honestly. Shut your eyes again, pet. Give me a moment to re-position myself."

A confused and nervous Dani had no notion of what was going on with her boyfriend. But suddenly she did!

"Okay, you can look now."

She didn't immediately catch Phil's entire proposal, but her autopilot had already kicked-in and said, "YES! Yes, yes, yes!"

From the other side of the ward came loud applause. After the hullabaloo had died down Phil naively asked, "If it's a boy, what should we call him?"

Quick as a flash Dani replied, "Well, for sure Mr Shawcross, it won't be..." she took a breath for comic effect. "Volvo!"

They both laughed as she leant across and wrapped him in her arms. They laughed again... They hugged again. He winced.


END

# A LEAP of FAITH

# Killing Time

My name is Sandy Hayes and I'm just killing time. I'm awaiting the arrival of the Scottish ferry. I'm a one-time resident of this ferry port town who has found himself comfortably early for the uplifting of my party of foot passengers. That being so I thought I would drop by the nearby yacht club – I was once a member there – and chance coming across an old face or two before duty calls.

However a small flaw has presented itself. I find myself denied entrance to the said club by an automatic gate. A gate which is closed; locked? So I cogitate, what are my options? Well, I could kill more time by reading the plethora of notices posted on the gate. Perhaps bellow a couple of 'hello's' or even sound my horn. Perhaps I'll ring some of my contact phone numbers. No, I'd likely find no takers. *So, what now Sandy?* I find myself having a conversation with my dashboard as I've no desire to embark on a touristy run down the

Antrim Coast road or offer a knowledgeable nod to the remains of the Olderfleet Castle ruins which tower above me and overlook the yacht club. No, it's the call of a cool pint which holds priority. "And I know the very place."

# Reminiscing

I'm very aware of the afternoon sun washing across my back. So relaxing. This is coupled with a growing anticipation of an expertly presented pint of stout, poured and delivered by chatty Kevin. He's the sole barman on duty at The Olderfleet bar. An opening slurp of the black liquid immediately registers me at peace with the world. Now I slip into some serious reminiscing. Another slurp and I've morphed into that boy sprinting along the adjacent road in an attempt to outrun the closing of a monstrous level-crossing barrier and the approaching boat train.

Alas, both the barrier and the train sit square across Olderfleet road, my route is effectively blocked. No one hears my inner cry of frustration. No one is interested. *I need to get through. I need to catch the Islandmagee ferry.* Gulping air the young Sandy is forced to reassess his options. The barrier – train and terminus – he knows aren't for moving anytime soon. His only option therefore is to sprint around the obstruction.

Sandy runs parallel to the terminus or big shed as it is known locally while keeping an eye out for old Jimmy, the harbour master. At the same time he is aware of trip hazards under-foot all along the quayside, which he has now entered. A hard left, and another turn sees him enter the terminus itself. Passing Mrs Doig's kiosk, he waves. Then at full tilt and parallel to the problem train, he makes for the exit. Outside he takes a moment to draw in new breath while leaning against the wall of Kelly's Coal office. Pushing off, young legs pumping like pistons quickly get him back up to speed. His target has also come into view.

# The Islandmagee Ferry

Frantically waving his arms, Sandy shouts, "NO—WAIT." Not a great start to Sandy's day, a day which already he fears is rapidly falling apart. Worse, crewman Sammy McCalmont has commenced the casting-off procedure! Dougie Hood is poised by the tiller... the ferryboat is slipping away from its elderly slipway.

***

Slipping down on his seat, he adjusts back to the upright and Sandy Hayes finds himself back in the present. A reflex hand prevents the spilling of his sacred pint thus avoiding crotch stained Chinos. Blearily he looks around in a 'did anyone notice kind-a way'? Several couples a few tables away appear to be giggling while a trio of harbour workers in another corner just shake their all-knowing heads. Sandy however, still only half awake, remains an easy catch and consequently is snatched back in into his reminiscences. He's gone again...

***

Closing in on the ferry slipway, Sandy continues with his furious flapping in an attempt to draw attention to his plight – he must not miss that boat! His [love] life depends on it. He hollers, "Dougie— DOUGIE. Sammy— SAMMY wait, wait for me." Facing up to the fact that his cries are lost within the industry of a busy harbour he picks up the pace as if a gold medal is at stake. The fact is that *she* is on board. She. His principal driver. But so is Billy King and he is after her too.

Sandy has reached the Islandmagee ferryboat terminal – a fine name for a battered ex-shipping container crudely fitted out with slatted seats and an ancient stove. Maintaining full throttle he hangs a right onto and down the slipway towards the ferry. Sandy's eyes are now focused on the tarnished thirty-five feet of open motorboat. More so, the exact spot where his leap of faith must land him. As he lunches towards the vessel he catches sight of Siobhan; her large almond eyes are eclipsed by a gaping mouth. In fact all of the passengers huddled within that ferryboat have developed similar expressions.

Too late! Young Sandy's feet have already left the slipway as the all-seeing Dougie manoeuvres his craft back into a position to receive 'late cargo'. Whether it was the sea swell running along the harbour quays or the turbulence within the hollowed out inlet from where the ferry operates, but the boy's actual trajectory and his planned route had differed somewhere between going airborne and landing on the ferry – aircraft carrier style, he finds himself skidding along the elderly ferryboat's starboard gunwale...

# Further Reminiscing

Again Sandy Hayes has found himself back in the present. He is also conscious of a recurring tenderness in his rear-end. Whether it can be attributed to general bad posture or that boyhood leap of faith, he's not sure. Either way he still remains eternally grateful to the owner of that big gnarled hand with grease encrusted fingernails and a vice-like grip. It had saved him from a would-be embarrassing bath in Larne harbour. However the up side was that he had been planted onto the ferry's wooden thwart right beside her. Equally, although it was a 'hard' landing – he felt like crying – finding himself beside her played a major part in holding back the tears. *So sore!*

Another swirl of a half-full glass coupled with a vigorous shake of his head, Sandy has noticed how things have changed around here. How the harbour has been remodelled to meet modern needs of a cross channel ro-ro ferry route – it's no masterpiece.

The big wooden terminus shed is long gone, replaced by a red brick and metal-clad structure of modern (ugly) design. Gone too is Mrs Doig's kiosk, the level crossing and the Kelly offices. No more huge stacks of loose coal and no more Kelly coal boats. No more shiploads of timber destined for the Curran Saw Mills. No more the once beautiful bay where he and the lads used to swim. No more small yachts swinging from moorings or clinker planked punts anchored to retrieval lines. No more Dougie, Sammy or their Islandmagee ferry. All gone and buried under mega-tonnes of infill and undulating tarmac and concrete. Sandy takes another slurp, but the remaining contents taste sour. He checks his watch, pushes the near empty glass to the side while slipping back for a final glimpse of times past, and that one boyhood adventure in particular.

Back onboard the open ferry boat the young Sandy remembers Sammy patting his mop of blond hair while nodding to Dougie, who shook his head and mumbled, "Wee lads, huh, they think they're indestructible."

With that rare comment, Dougie had tightened down his white (ish) cap, knocked the engine into reverse and throttled up. Meanwhile, as Sandy is dealing with his throbbing back-side, he also notices Billy's mocking sneer. He is seated on the port-side of the ferry and close to the bow, opposite Siobhan. As Sandy continues to rearrange himself, she slips her arm over his shoulder whispering, "You OK wee fella?" His inner voice chirps up, *Whea-hay! You'll not forget this in a hurry lad!* Dropping his head to disguise his blushes he catches a glimpse of the Billy boy glaring at him. Sandy is trying not to smile. He can almost hear the grinding of Billy's teeth, even over the reverberations of the ancient engine bouncing off the underside of the commercial quay.

With the ferry safely clear of nautical commerce Dougie expertly spins the craft setting his course towards Islandmagee. The voyage has begun but a nor' easterly breeze is building. Spray breaks over the bow as Siobhan crouches down behind Sandy. Neither her, Sandy or Billy had even thought of packing an anorak. *Oh dear, it's all getting a bit roly-poly out here.* Sandy, being a seasoned sailor, pretends not to be bothered by the gyrations of the ferry. Siobhan continues to observe the wild life circling the ferryboat. In the same moment, a glance towards his arch enemy (at least for the day) confirms that Billy has turned somewhat pale!

Sandy's inner voice chirps up again. *Hold it together son — you're all right, not feeling one bit queasy so you're not; not queasy at all. ...Need to impress Siobhan.*

She however has turned her sights towards the fading Billy King. She makes it clear that she is not impressed by Sandy's mocking of Billy.

With the love pendulum swinging away from him, Sandy unveils his caring side by advising his mate to focus on the horizon, or at least the slipway destination, saying, "Come on Billy boy, stand up. Big breaths."

Truth be told, Sandy wasn't feeling too great himself. But he was instantly cured as a lock of Siobhan's long auburn hair brushed across his face; the lingering scent of Siobhan had wrapped around him.

Now, having docked on the lee-side of the Islandmagee slipway the dozen or so passengers faced the prospect of dodging the sizeable waves breaking and washing across the concrete. Sammy physically held the craft close to the slipway as his passengers departed. Sandy took his chance; over the side in a flash, but poor timing found him up to his ankles in the breaking swell. He in turn held out a supportive arm to his girl who had already removed her shoes and socks. Billy however, was the problem. Hesitating, he was one of the final folk to disembark.

Finally, phase two of their outing was underway, late but underway. Privately, Sandy reflected, *Huh, if I'd got my backside out of bed in time this morning there would have been no need for all my sprinting, dare-devil leaping and ... the landing on my tail. Oh my arse is killing me. All I was after was a hand-in-hand dander to Ferris's bay — but hey wait, hasn't she still got her arm around me; woo-hoo!* Then, just to spoil the moment his dreaded inner voice spoke again, *Agh, sure Sandy, she's just feeling sorry for you, you know, like a big sister would.* "Agh, bugger off you."

Siobhan suddenly rigid, asks Sandy, "What did you just say?"

Quick as a flash Sandy causally answers, "Na, nothin'. It's just my backside. Sooo sore!

Sniggering, Siobhan delivers a playful slap to the area in question while offering, "Want me to rub it?"

Sandy, blushing, glances away. Looking back over his shoulder, down the narrow road towards the slipway. He picks out the Billy boy who has it seems given up on the chase. He has remained by the slipway and looks as if he's taking the return ferry home.

A smirking Sandy quietly announces, "No contest." But she hears him.

She delivers another smack to his backside, harder this time, while saying, "Don't push your luck wee fella. Right, come on then, I'll race you to the top and then we'll decide if it's a no contest." With that she was off ... he had been challenged.

# Real Time

Approaching the surface of real time once again, Sandy has become aware of tannoy announcements, clanging and loud bleeping noises. He literally jumps out of his seat. From his beer garden he was more or less opposite to where the blue and white P&O ferry nosed into its berth.

"Ah, that's me on the move." But he dithered. Toilets first. Pints, can't handle them anymore. Should have known better.

Striding away from the 'fleet bar, the rustling of trees and the whistling of fibre wires alerts him. "Heck there's a quare auld breeze blowing, must have been a right rough crossing."

*Poor kids, hope they're ok. Ah, for sure my Siobhan'll have had them well couched. She was always a great traveller and far better than me. Regardless of the weather and whether she would be helming a sailboat or braving the ocean on a cruise liner my Mrs would be in her element. Oh happy days: Ferris bay, the town parks and the night time walks along the Promenade and oh, those hops. Yes, happy days indeed back then...*

With big smiles and waving arms the Hayes family gathering gained momentum. Daughter, Niamh lead the chase followed by Granny Siobhan with Granddaughter, Grainne on her right hand and her wee grandson, Fin on her left. More kisses flowed for Grandpa Sandy as they marched towards his Hyundai SUV.

Driving home that afternoon Sandy's thoughts drifted between his rear view mirror vision of daughter and grandkids and his rear view memories of that crossing on that Islandmagee ferry.

That was where in many ways the romance between him and Siobhan O'Loane took root leading to their marriage some decades later.

"Ah, where does the time go?" Sandy said aloud.

"Keep you eye's on the road ye auld eejit. What did you say anyway?" was his wife's reply.

His daughter then added her comment, "Ah ma, give daddy a break, the poor man has had to endure that old 'fleet bar all day and no doubt he has been drowning in an overture of reminiscing."

Sandy said nothing, but he leant upwards and released the weight off his backside, before settling again. Comfortable.

END

# A NOT SO TENDER TRAP

# Fuengirola

Number 69, The Avenue is the home of the Buchanan's. Billy (68) and Lilly (64). Billy is a retired builder, Lilly a retired civil servant. They've done well for themselves during their forty years of marriage. Late last year he sold his business and she commenced her early retirement plan. As well as Number 69 they owned various rental properties around Margate and Hearne Bay. A sizeable villa in Fuengirola completes their portfolio. It was here that Billy and Lilly found themselves being eased into the general Marbella lifestyle.

Back home in Kent and within walking distance of Number 69 lived Alec and Elisabeth O'Leary. Bizarrely they had first met Billy and Lilly while queuing for the same flight to Spain. Needless to say a neighbourly friendship was kindled. Although they don't have any foreign property owning credentials, the well-off and childless O'Leary's typically planed their annual holiday to fit between the Malaga golf courses and the uber-wealthy Puerto Banús yachting scene: Alec is a golf devote, his wife, not so. Boutiques, sun bathing and drooling over the never ending register of super yachts were among Elisabeth's day-time pursuits.

Back on home turf Elisabeth (40 ish) and Alec (38) had been added to the Buchanan's guest list whether they be large or intimate functions. Similarly, holiday calendars allowing, they would be top of the Fuengirola guest list too. Occasionally these functions could become quite raunchy. Liz (as she preferred to be called) took a dim view of her husband's enthusiasm for such occasions. His habitual breast watching really boiled her blood.

Frequently this could lead to either Liz's early departure or the dragging off of Alec before something happened. Both Billy and Lilly remained sympathetic, knowing well the reason for an O'Leary non-appearance. Billy especially would be quietly disappointed as he carried a bit of torch for Liz. He often fantasised after her. Over the years, Lilly had turned a blind eye to *her* husband's apparent obsession with the opposite sex. She would regularly accuse him of being an over-aged dirty git, a voyeur in the making. She was no angel either...

Then there was the Malaga based couple Simone and Max Martinez who were also high on the Buchanan's Spanish guest list. He, a Spanish national was a high flying entrepreneur. She managed several of his business outlets. They were very much a product of the in-set. Simone was of Asian descent, tall yet petite of figure, her boyish hair style emphasised her facial profile, hazel eyes, impish nose and luscious lips – she was indeed a head turner. Max stood about six foot two, well-toned. Facially he sported a stubble beard. Often he pulled his hair into a pony tail – he was in many ways the epitome of the Spanish toy-boy. Simone was the quiet one, well until the sangria loosened her inhibitions. When they were at home they shared a property within the same urbanisation as the Buchanan's.

# Anniversary Party

One moon-lit night at Billy and Lily's Fuengirola villa in mid-August the occasion for celebration was the Buchanan's ruby anniversary. Billy and Lilly had been toiling all day – it would be a large gathering, ex-Pats generally and golfing friends fostered via the neighbouring five star Country Club and Spa. Neither Billy nor Lilly played, but together they talked a good game. Billy could hold his own on a variety of topics, especially the world of English beers. Lilly lived for the spa, gym and her monthly massages. It had been a particularly hot Mediterranean day. Even so, undeterred Alec O'Leary was out on the course. Liz however, had opted to lend Lilly some assistance with the party decor as well as discussing the finer detail of the evening's plan should Alec over-step the line.

Tables were set up around the garden. Billy's home-made self-service bars were stocked and the catering company was working in tandem with Lilly – no menu request was too difficult. The BBQs together with a huge paella pan were positioned and readied for lighting at an appropriate time. Indoors, endless dips and cheeses had been prepared and jugs of sangria were chilling. Billy's final task of the day was to hang strings of outdoor lights and place coloured up-lighters to best show off Lilly's garden after sunset. His centre piece was a nine and half foot long fibre-glass sailing dinghy filled to the gunwales with various bottles of English beer imported especially for the occasion. As for the girls, sangria tasting was the order of their day

"Got to keep the body hydrated" was Lilly's call.

Liz was feeling quite tipsy already but remained conscious of the time. She'd half agreed to meet Alec for pre-party cocktails down by the beach.

The hosts too had found time to exercise their own pre-function chilling routines: Billy had planted himself in the pool's shallow end. Bottle in hand and his BBC Spanish Phrase Book and Dictionary in the other. Billy always liked to prepare. Lilly however, had driven off towards the spa where a pre-booked masseur would be in waiting to work his magic on her taught limbs.

# A Set Up?

Later, after a couple of cocktails in their holiday villa, Liz could not disguise her querying smile as an excited husband went about the business of prettying himself. It seemed he'd changed his party outfit a dozen times. Conversely and at her first attempt she'd chosen a plunging black number. Very daring for Liz, but if it kept her husband under control with eyes principally for her, it would be worth it. As for the throng of guests that she and Alec were preparing to mingle with, Liz realised she had no control over them ...*and anyway, it might be nice to be a focus of attention for once.*

As he finally emerged from their en suite shower she felt somehow aroused by the sight of his mostly tanned dripping wet body. Holding her grin she was visualising him as her toy-boy, and she wanted things to stay that way. Easing herself off the bed and standing up straight, shoulders back, she slowly, provocatively, raised her head thus showing off *her* toned body. As Alec moved closer she noticed a certain twinkle in his eyes. She knew what was coming next! She did not resist as the little black number fell to the floor...

***

With the passion diluted, Liz teasingly pushed him away, saying, "That's what happens when you're a good boy." She leaned in again and kissed him. He pulled her closer. She wriggled free, continuing with her lecture. "Understand? Now come on, no more messing. We need to get dressed for this bloody party. OK?"

Suddenly it was Liz's turn to be indecisive. The little plunging black number got ditched in favour of a full length red and green flower patterned summer dress. She'd also replaced sandals for red sky-scraper heels.

For Alec's final choice it was back to the black shirt over white pants. With final mirror inspections done and security alarms keyed, the O'Leary's closed and triple locked their uPVC front door. Hand-in-hand they strolled towards the ruby celebrations. He held the gift, she, the flowers.

"You're very quiet my dear." said Alec expecting an immediate reply, but none came. He continued, sniggering, "Did I hit the spot earlier?" He stopped, turned and kissed Liz.

She pulled away. "Alec, behave – people could be watching" She smacked his backside. "Naughty boy."

"Well?' he asked.

"Oh, just dreaming big boy. Look, look at that moon for goodness sake." But it was more than that. She was running the plan through her brain again. Alec had no clue what was hatching.

# Some Things Never Change

As Alec pushed open the Buchanan's gate, Liz froze. However, before she could make a retreat, another two couples had arrived. Lilly had also appeared to welcome everyone. Sensing Liz's dilemma, Lilly wrapped a supportive arm around her while raving about her dress choice. "Oh darling you look sensational – the movie star, no less. It'll be you we'll need to watch tonight." Nonplussed, Alex just looked on.

Not long after, Max and Simone appeared. He wore a tropical patterned shirt tucked into cream linen trousers while Simone had poured herself into a tight, plunging, black top over white knee-length pants.

Without warning Liz said, "Oh hey look Alex, look at Simone. You could be tonight's black and white twins." Alec said nothing. He just sipped his sangria while his eyes covertly scanned for flesh.

The majority of the guests had arrived with much cheek-to-cheek kissing and endless '...oh darlings...'.

Music played loudly, the party was in full swing; dancing, singing and consuming an endless supply of alcohol. The compact garden appeared to be at capacity as Billy opened the bi-fold doors to give access to the lounge and a fabulous spread of food. Everything was going swimmingly – in fact a few of the younger couples had taken to the swimming pool.

Alec was getting restless... His offer to fetch food for his wife was accepted – not unlike a Linford off, he was out of the blocks on the B of the bang and was soon into the throng. As best she could, Liz continued to watch her husband until he got swallowed up out of sight. Just as she was upping to search for him, Simone joined her.

They strolled towards the pool's deep-end in the quieter area of the Buchanan's garden. They sat by a stunning flood-lit deep purple flowering Bougainvillea. As they chatted Simone placed a hand on Liz's shoulder and said; "Darling Liz, do you *really* want to go through with this?"

Liz turned away to gaze back towards the main body of the gathering. She was scanning, hoping, Alec would be trotting back to her with plate in hand. Suddenly she caught a glimpse of him. Not surprisingly he was flirting with one of the younger party goers. "Yes."

# Call to Action

Despite her answer, a dithering Liz found herself questioning the plan hatched earlier in the week. In a whisper she asked herself what future could there be if her husband was caught red-handed cheating on her, again? Her thoughts were interrupted by Simone.

"A cheating bastard. Yes, no?"

The two of them stared at each other. Eventually Liz gave Simone the go ahead but stressed that she must be sure that it was him making the moves – driving things. "Understand?" demanded Liz.

Simone nodded. "Understood boss," she said quietly before slipping back into the throng.

A deep breathing Liz stood tall, portraying the confident lady that most folk took her for. She knew it was a front. Feeling nauseous and without drawing undue attention to herself, she made haste for one of the villa's bathrooms.

***

A knock on the bathroom door shocked her back to reality. A quick facial check, a light application of her Chanel Rouge Allure Luminous pink lipstick and the smallest nail-full of scoops brought the colour back into her cheeks. Liz O'Leary was ready to face whatever she needed to on the other side of that door. The click of the barrel bolt aligned with an instant smile. Her next stop would be the paella pan.

***

A hunger had suddenly filled her. She couldn't help herself though, she had to have a sneak peek into the dimly lit room which was doubling as the dance hall. Sure enough Alec was on top form, getting close up and personal with Simone.

With a shake of her head she instantly turned away, *bastard* she thought. So focused on the goings on she hadn't realised that *she* was being asked to dance.

"Oh, no, no, sorry, I'm just heading for the paella … sorry, maybe later?"

It seemed like forever, but eventually the exclamation came from the direction of the dimly lit dance floor.

Alec dashed past her, "OH HELLS TEETH, SHE'S NOT A SHE. FUCK ME … SHE'S A BLOODY HE — AGH!"

It was an embarrassed Alec O'Leary who looked directly into his wife's eyes before turning and stumbling into the hole he had just dug for himself! In doing so he had knocked into her plate. He stopped, turned and having exchanged his guilt ridden persona for tearful puppy dog eyes, he looked towards Liz for instant forgiveness. Alas, all he caught was his smirking wife.

Confused, he said, "HOME. It's eh, time we were away."

"Nope, not for me honey — my party has just begun. Hope you've learnt your lesson. Tomorrow … we'll talk. We'll seriously talk." Liz turned and walked away, thinking, *Now, where is that young chap from earlier?*

Simone quietly emerged from the scene of the set-up. Finding Liz, she asked if she wanted to hear the details.

"I'd rather not, well not just now. Well, other than… did *he* actually—"

"No, not flesh on flesh so to speak but enough groping for him to realise that the girl Simone is in fact the boy Simon."

***

Liz stayed over at the Buchanan villa that evening but sleep eluded her. She rose with the morning sun as the rest of the villa slept on. Wrapped in a bath robe the dew tickled the soles of her bare feet and she opted to paddle on the steps of the glassy pool. While still soaking up the dawn chorus, Lilly dressed in Billy's England top and pants appeared with bowls of breakfast fruits. She asked, "Need anything stronger my darling, you had a terrible night."

Liz replied almost in a whisper; "No, no, this is fine." Then with tears in her eyes she added, "You know, you and Billy, and of course Simone, have been wonderful and I'm so sorry to have spoiled your party. So now, once I've showered and of course demolished this fruit, I will be away, out of your hair to *demolish* that idiot of a husband of mine. Once my toy-boy. Joke! I think the final few days of our annual Spanish sojourn will be ... a quiet affair."

# One Year Later...

Billy and Lilly have sold 69 The Avenue together with various other UK ventures. They've moved lock stock and barrel to Spain but remain in the snail-like process of finding a smaller but higher end development. Costa Brava way possibly, Barcelona maybe. Lilly remains as lively as ever, but Billy is having a series of scans. Max and Simone have also moved on, but further afield. He is involved in a covert real estate development somewhere in Kuala Lumpur – possibly dodgy with overtures of money-laundering. Simone/Simon remains in Spain having undergone major surgery. In parallel with her convalescing, Simone has signed on with an online university degree course.

***

On the morning after the ruby party, Liz found herself staring at a half open front door. Bare footed she tentatively moved along the marble hall. No sound, no

signs of her philandering husband. Suddenly a foreboding draped itself over her. Whispering she asked
herself, "Oh good God. Jeez, Mary and Joseph, what
the hell has he done?"

The lounge door was ajar – but no Alec. Then Liz
became aware of groaning from further up the hall.
Tentatively she eased the door of the bathroom open,
where upon lay her husband. The sight and smell of
him made her gag. A rancid cocktail of urine, vomit
and spirits assailed her nostrils.. Her eyes took in the
stained trousers half-on-half-off, and legs half out of
the bath. It was amusing, and sad.

Aghast, she turned away as he hopelessly gazed up
at her. Then to make matters worse a broken bottle of
Jack Daniels attacked her feet.

"Aaaah!" It was too late. A trickle of red soon
joined the congealed and stained floor. Finally, and before making her exit, she rammed on the cold shower.
Walking away towards their pool, Liz O'Leary shook
her head and issued one final word, "Pathetic!"

Once home in Kent things had continued to be
tense in the O'Leary household. Alec had moved out.
Liz and he remain estranged, both however are attending counselling...


END

# Acknowledgements

I trust that you've enjoyed this my fourth book of fiction and whilst I sign myself off as the author, no piece of work is doable without 'a back room' team – those souls who keep me on the straight and narrow. Some are aware of their contribution others, not so. Nevertheless I say a grateful thank you

Take for example the opening story *First timer*. This was a tale of Darren, a youthful lad taking his first naive steps into the world of after-work outings; 'boys chasing girls chasing boys'. The basis of the story was conceived during many conversations with my friend of many years, the musician Esler Burke. Reminiscing, we shared the calamities and the odd success in our search for romance via the shop floor...

*Twisted Elbow* however was a different challenge for me. If you've read any of my previous three novels you will have noticed my addiction to all things nautical. For me *'Elbow'* was a step into the relative unknown –

OK, the worlds of motorsport and competitive sailing quite often run in parallel, such is my connection, but only at an armchair level: Formula One, rally-cross, auto testing and of course, the hill-climb scene. So I reckoned that the basics of a motorsport competition can't differ too much from racing a performance sailboat. Nah!

My thanks are due to Larne Motor Club: in particular to their Chairman John Millar, as well as Kenny O'Neill and Secretary, Lucy Whitford. More thanks are passed to Laurence Martin and former British auto-test champion, William Rutherford. Together they gave of their time to explain the ins and outs of car types and pointed me in the direction of one of the hill climb greats, Mike Pilbeam. This man was also so helpful in all aspects of motorsport. He agreed with my choice of car – a Pilbeam MP68 Vrage – for what had been a tricky writing challenge. It seems now that I may have to adjust my strap-line from Nautical Novelist to *Nautical and Motorsport Novelist...* I can still taste the afterburn of high octane fuel.

*Leap of Faith*. I cannot deny that this tale is as close as it comes to a biography. Yes of course some names have been changed! However, beneath this storyline morphed my private protest against the then annihilation of the once beautiful harbour area of my port town: Curran Point along to Ship Street, Coastguard and Olderfleet Roads, by an expanding and ruthless harbour company of that time. Agh! *Leap of Faith* remains one of my favourite wee stories; it first appeared in a Mid and East Antrim council's funded anthology entitled; *Shaped by the Sea.*

Finally, *A Not So Tender Trap* was for me a semi-sarcastic tale of just rewards for a much down trodden and disrespected wife who had found herself trapped in a male dominated world. Back then it seemed the male of the species had created the rule book (it was a blank document) in respect of how a girlfriend or wife should be treated. ...misogamy is the word which comes to mind.

Finally, and as I've mentioned in all of my previous writings, none of this would be remotely possible without the support and space created by my talented artist wife Jane, and the immediate family.

# Also by Thomas Jobling

The Big Event
Champions & High Achievers
Chasing Shadows
Arthur's Dead
A Letter to a Lucky Man

As well as his novels, **Chasing Shadows, Arthur's Dead** and **A Letter to a Lucky Man**, Thomas Jobling has contributed to a book of thirteen short stories produced by Larne Writers Group (now renamed East Antrim Writers Group), entitled, *13*, The print run sold out, and the proceeds were forwarded to the Marie Curie Foundation. Tom's contribution was *First Timer*.

A more recent project, **Shaped by the Sea** is an anthology of creative writing past and present, driven by another Larne author, Angeline King.

Tom's contributions were the short story, **Leap of Faith** and a [very] short poem which found its way onto the front cover. Hosted by Mid & East Antrim Council as part of their St.Art programme, the ***Shaped by the Sea*** project was funded by the European Union's Peace IV initiative. The finished work is bound beautifully as a book of short stories, historical pieces, poems, rhymes and songs, together with reproduced paintings by local artists.

# About The Author

Based in the Northern Irish, County Antrim port town of Larne, Thomas Jobling is a retired businessman, an experienced yachtsman and nautical scribe turned novelist.

His debut novel, *Chasing Shadows* was published in 2014, and achieved success with readers from within the nautical world of competitive sailing. His second novel, again with a strong maritime backdrop, *Arthur's Dead,* was a thrilling but tragic love story and received very positive reviews, from as far away as Australia via their leading yachting magazine *Afloat.* His third novel, *A Letter to a Lucky Man* (2020) is, according to the columnist, Dave Selby, *not merely a deftly plotted read-at-one-sitting thriller, but a warm and human, rite of passage tale that charts the journey of a boy to mature adulthood.*

Prior to these works, Thomas had written a 'how-to' planning and management e-manual designed to assist with the organisation of sailing regattas and championship level events. Such was the popularly of *The Big Event* that it earned the badge of a 'best practice' document with both the Royal Yachting Association and the Irish Sailing Association.

A subsequent publication, *Champions & High Achievers*, charts the 'great and the good' from the 1950 inception of the East Antrim Boat Club on Larne Lough, up to 2013. It can be found on the club's website at www.eabc.club.

Having been born by the sea, boats and boating were destined to become companions of Thomas's and he continues to enjoy his passion for all things afloat. Going freelance in the early seventies, he covered the marine scene by reporting sailboat events for the leading UK and Irish yachting magazines as well as writing weekly columns for his local papers. However, marriage and an expanding family demanded that he found 'real' employment! To back-up his scribing he found himself building glass-fibre yachts, leading on to involvement with the plastics distribution business before moving into the construction industry selling plastic building products. Several decades later he had risen to the level of national sales manager.

He has competed at the highest level within the sport of sailboat racing. Currently he races a quarter-tonner type of yacht, but at a more leisurely pace. During this period he also found time to serve as his club's Commodore, and thereafter as President of the Irish GP14 Association while he and wife Jane raised their family of three; two boys and a girl.

Having taken early retirement from business he quickly rekindled and re-developed his writing craft within the world of creative writing. There are therefore, many more tales lurking within the head of author, Thomas Jobling...

Follow him on Facebook, Twitter and LinkedIn… and more especially source out your copy of a Thomas Jobling novel.

**Enjoy.**

www.ingramcontent.com/pod-product-compliance
Lightning Source LLC
Chambersburg PA
CBHW040229170726
48295CB00014B/861